From Mom
To Gramma
To Granddaugter

May we all
cherish the
beautifue swan (soul)
within us,
7/29/08

Bethany Joy
a circle
of Love
Joy Harvey
Zoe Rosemary

*For James and his animals* ➤ B.S.

*For my parents*
*And with thanks to Chris Lewin and the Hurlburt family* ➤ W.M.

Text copyright © 1995 by Brenda Seabrooke
Illustrations copyright © 1995 by Wenhai Ma

First edition 1995

Library of Congress Cataloging-in-Publication Data

Seabrooke, Brenda.
The swan's gift / Brenda Seabrooke; illustrated by Wenhai Ma. — 1st ed.
Summary: A farmer whose crops have failed because of drought cannot
bear to shoot a beautiful magic swan, even to feed his starving family.
ISBN 1-56402-360-5
[1. Fairy tales.] I. Ma, Wenhai, ill. II. Title.
PZ8.S323Sw   1994
[E]—dc20   94-41788

2 4 6 8 10 9 7 5 3 1

Printed in Hong Kong

The pictures in this book were done in
watercolor and pencil.

Candlewick Press
2067 Massachusetts Avenue
Cambridge, Massachusetts 02140

# THE *Swan's Gift*

BRENDA SEABROOKE

illustrated by

WENHAI MA

CANDLEWICK PRESS
CAMBRIDGE, MASSACHUSETTS

Anton was a farmer who lived with his wife Rubina and their seven children at the edge of a forest. He worked hard and they were happy for many years. Then one spring the rains didn't fall and Anton's wheat died in the fields.

➤ As winter came on, their
food supply grew smaller and
smaller.

Soon Anton's shoulders were
stooped with worry. Rubina's
plump apple cheeks withered.
The children no longer sang or
laughed or danced, for they
were all too hungry.

❧ Every day Anton went out to look for game but returned without firing a shot. And every day Rubina added water to the onion soup until there was nothing in the pot but water. When Anton saw his family crying with hunger he wanted to cry too. But instead he took his gun and went out again into the cold cold night.

➼ He had to find something for them to eat, a bird or a rabbit. But the black branches were empty of birds and no rabbits crouched in the frozen brush. The only tracks Anton saw were his own.

He came to a small hill and knew it was the last one he would be able to climb before his strength was gone. His feet were numb and his breath rasped in the freezing air. At the top of the rise he stopped to rest, scanning the snow for animal tracks.

❧ In despair Anton turned to go. Just then he saw below him a lake that had not yet frozen over. Its edge was lacy with ice and at its center floated a swan of such dazzling beauty that Anton could not look away. Its stark white feathers gleamed against the dark water and as Anton watched, the swan seemed to grow larger until its image filled his eyes.

➤ Suddenly juices flowed into Anton's mouth. He could taste succulent roast swan and see his children's faces glowing as his family sat at the table eating again. He raised his gun and sighted down the long barrel.

Anton put his finger on the trigger. The swan seemed to be looking at him, listening for the shot that would kill it.

➢ He lowered the gun. The swan was the most beautiful creature Anton had ever seen. As he watched, the swan fanned its magnificent wings in a way that seemed to embrace the night. Anton closed his eyes and thought of his family. Again he raised the gun.

✸ Hours seemed to pass. The feathers on the swan's breast moved gently with each beat of its heart, and Anton could feel his own heart beating. He lifted his heavy wet feet, walked a few steps, and then dropped to his knees.

"I can't do it," he said.

"Why not?" asked a voice as soft as snow or feathers ruffling in a gentle wind.

"I cannot kill beauty. If I kill this swan my family will have food for one or two meals. And then what? We will be hungry again and it will have been for nothing."

Anton was too tired to be surprised that he was speaking to the swan or the wind or the night. He was too tired to walk back home. He bowed his head with sadness for his family.

➤ With a cry the swan lifted its
wings, rose from the lake, and
circled over Anton, water dropping
from its wing feathers. As the water
hit the snow it froze into crystals
that sparkled in the moonlight.
Anton reached out and touched
one. It was hard, harder than ice,
and did not melt in the warmth
of his hand.

"A diamond!" Anton said.

Quickly he scooped up the
diamonds that lay in a glittering
circle around him. He filled his
pockets with them and set off
through the snow to a nearby
village.

❧ Anton was no longer tired. He no longer felt the cold. He woke up the innkeeper, calling, "I need food."

"Your crops failed," said the innkeeper. "Everyone knows you have no money."

"I have a diamond," said Anton.

"Where would the likes of you get a diamond?" the man scoffed.

"Let me in and I will explain."

The innkeeper fed Anton cold venison and sweet dumplings while Anton told his story, and the innkeeper's wife packed him a sled with roast chickens and cheeses and beets. Then they sent Anton on his way so that they could begin looking for the magic swan themselves.

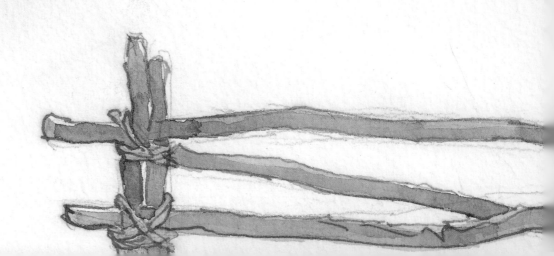

➤ Rubina met him at the door. "Did you find any game? Mischa has fainted."

"No. But look what I have brought." Anton showed her the sled.

"But how did you get it?" she asked.

For answer, he spilled the diamonds onto the table.

"Oh," cried Rubina, "you have turned to robbery!"

"No," said Anton. And he told her all about the swan and how it had circled him with diamonds falling from its wings.

❧ Anton and Rubina woke the children even though it was the middle of the night, and they all sat at the table eating slowly, enjoying the flavor of the food and the wonderful feeling in their stomachs. Rubina's black eyes sparkled as she filled her children's bowls. Anton felt his strength returning. Several of the children hummed as they were put to bed.

✦ Anton and Rubina and their children prospered, for they used their diamonds wisely and well. News of the magic swan spread throughout the land and many people searched for it. But the swan was never found.

Sometimes when Anton was alone in the forest the image of the swan rose before him. He saw again the gleam of its feathers, the coral glow of its beak, and the magnificent reach of its wings as it glided silently across the sky.